WALT DISNEY'S
BABES in TOYLAND

By Barbara Shook Hazen
Based on the Walt Disney motion picture *Babes in Toyland*
Pictures by the Walt Disney Studio
Adapted by Earl and Carol Marshall

A GOLDEN BOOK • NEW YORK

rhcbooks.com

ISBN 978-0-7364-3879-7 (trade) — ISBN 978-0-7364-3880-3 (ebook)

Printed in the United States of America

10 9 8 7 6 5 4 3 2 1

"Look, Mary!" said Tom. "There's a bridge.
I wonder if that's the one."

Mary read, " 'To find the Toymaker, who
will decide your fate: First go down the ridge.
Then you'll find a bridge.' "

"Oh, it must be," she said. "It fits the
directions just perfectly."

"Yeah! Hooray!" shouted all the children, who were Mary's little brothers and sisters.

"I'm glad that we got lost in Toyland," said Little Boy Blue. "And I'm glad that the kind trees captured us, and that we never have to leave."

"Hurry! Let's go see the Toymaker!" said Bo-Peep.

On the other side of
the bridge was a tall
building with candy-
cane columns and ice
cream domes.

Little tin soldiers
stood by the gates, and
a floppy-eared dog
slept on the steps.

Tom knocked on the door. He rang
the doorbell. And three times he called,
"Anyone home?" Then Mary pointed to
a sign above a window.

The sign said:

TOYLAND
TOY FACTORY
CLOSED
for
ALTERATIONS
business
is not as usual
GENIUS AT WORK
INSIDE

Tom, Mary, and the children all crowded around the window. They could see two men inside. One had a sweet, gentle face.

"That must be the Toymaker," said Tom.

The other man was pointing excitedly at a huge object covered with blue velvet.

"I've got it! I've really got it this time," said Grumio, the Toymaker's helper.

"Got what?" asked the Toymaker.

"The greatest invention in the world," answered Grumio. "A toy-making machine!"

"All I know," said the Toymaker, "is that you have got to get to work. Do you know what time it is?"

"Half past October," answered Grumio. "That leaves us two and a half months before the Christmas deadline. And with my invention, we don't need half that time."

Grumio unveiled his machine.

"There!" he said. "Isn't it magnificent?"

"If it works," replied the Toymaker.

Sadly he thought of Grumio's other inventions,
all lying at the bottom of the Toyland scrap heap.

"Watch," said Grumio. He started putting things into the machine, singing as he did:

"*A touch of sugar, a dash of spice;*
Add a pinch of everything nice.
Cheeks of pink, eyes of blue;
Now add a ribbon, a bow, or two—
And I'm through."
He pulled the lever marked START.

START

Lights flashed.
Buzzers buzzed.
Wheels spun.
Churns churned
and dials turned.

In less time than it takes to say "Toyland," a
beautiful doll fell out of the slot marked FINISH.
"Amazing!" said the Toymaker.

"And that's not all," said Grumio. He showed the Toymaker how his machine could make

dollhouses

and squeaky mouses,

and balls

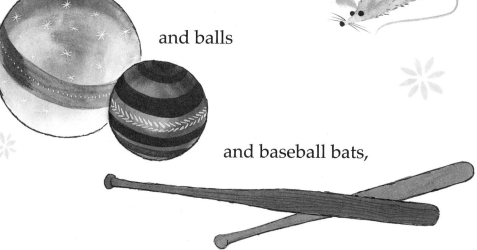

and baseball bats,

puzzle parts

and party hats,

alphabets

and rocket jets,

and toys not even
thought of yet!

"Wonderful!" said the Toymaker. "But we need millions of dolls and millions of alphabets, not just one or two."

"I know," said Grumio proudly. "And my machine *can* make millions of toys at a time."

"Bravo!" cried the Toymaker. He quickly pinned some medals on Grumio.

Then the happy Toymaker started pressing buttons all over the machine.

He pulled all the levers for all kinds of toys—the ones marked GIRLS and the ones marked BOYS.

"Stop!" cried Grumio. "The machine will make millions of toys at a time. But it can only make *one kind at a time.*"

The warning came too late. Grumio couldn't move fast enough to stop the Toymaker.

The machine began to hum: *Chug-a-chug, blub-a-blub, bim-a-bam-a-BOOM! Chug-a-chug, zub-a-zub, zim-a-zam-a-ZOOM!*

Then it began to quiver.
Then it began to quake.
Then it really began to shake.
Then the smoke blew.
And the sparks flew.

A sign flashed:

QUITS

FIN

And the toy machine gave a great big groan, and broke into a million bits.

"Oh, oh, oh!" cried the Toymaker. "Now I'm really ruined."

"If only you had listened to me," groaned Grumio.

"Won't somebody please listen to *me*," said Tom, coming into the Toyshop. "My name is Tom Piper, and this is Mary. The trees told us to turn ourselves in to you. We and the children have been trying . . ."

"Children!" cried the Toymaker. "Don't you know the first rule of Toyland? *Children are never allowed to see the toys before Christmas.*"

"But there won't be any toys this Christmas," sighed Grumio.

"Oh yes there will," said Tom. "We'll all help. That is, if you agree, Mr. Toymaker."

"I not only agree," said the delighted Toymaker, "I sentence it as your fate!"

And a very happy fate it was for everyone.
All the children were given the task of working
on their favorite toys.

Little Boy Blue put the
button eyes on teddy bears.

And Wee Willie
Winkie put the rockers
on rocking chairs.

And Bo-Peep
made beanbags
shaped like pears.

Tom put the finished
toys in boxes.

Then Mary
wrapped everything
in yards of ribbons
and tissue paper.

And the happy Toymaker
put on the DON'T OPEN TILL
CHRISTMAS stickers.

Even Grumio helped. He gave up making machines and made beakers of pink lemonade instead.

And everyone thought him a truly great genius, because he made the best pink lemonade in Toyland.